Benita and the
NIGHT CREATURES

Barefoot Books would like to thank
Emily Golightly, Media Coordinator / Librarian
at Newport Elementary School, for her help
in the development of this book.

★ This title won the 2024 Pura Belpré
Honor Medal for the Spanish edition
published by Barefoot Books in 2023

Barefoot Books
23 Bradford Street, 2nd Floor
Concord, MA 01742

Graphic design
by Lindsey Leigh,
Barefoot Books
Edited and art directed
by Kate DePalma
and Bree Reyes,
Barefoot Books

Reproduction by
Bright Arts, Hong Kong
Printed in China
This book was typeset
in Grandstander,
Graphen, and
Monster Mash
The illustrations were
prepared with pencil
and digital techniques

ISBN 979-8-88859-346-2

Library of Congress
Cataloging-in-
Publication Data is
available under LCCN
2023932659

1 3 5 7 9 8 6 4 2

Benita and the NIGHT CREATURES

words by **Mariana Llanos**

art by **Cocoretto**

Barefoot Books
Step inside a story

Benita found a brand-new book to devour.
Excited, she opened the first page.

Cuco found a brand-new home to haunt.
Excited, he bounced in from the window and yelled,

"Boo!"

"Bless you," answered Benita,
with her nose buried in her book.

"*Booo!*"

screamed Cuco, and the tree
outside the window shivered.

"You too!"
Benita replied,
and she flipped
a page.

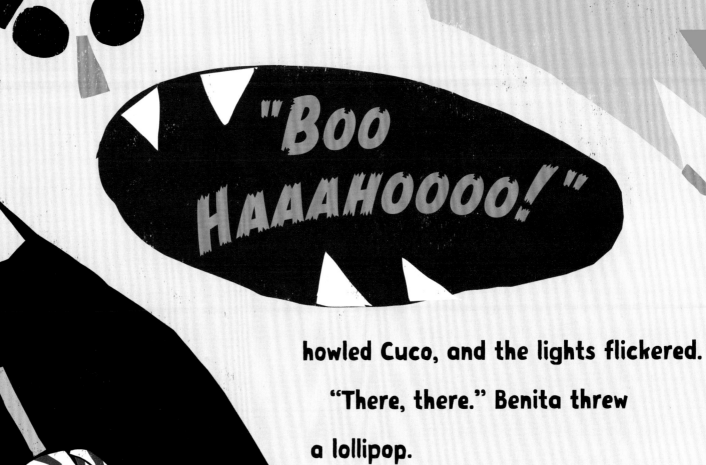

howled Cuco, and the lights flickered.

"There, there." Benita threw
a lollipop.

Cuco's jaw dropped. *Why
wasn't this child afraid?*

"I'm going to need help from
a friend," he said.

So, the next night . . .

"FEEEENNN!"

Tunche's breath froze the air.

"Hush, hush," Benita shushed.

"Quiet!" demanded Benita, her eyes glued to her book.

Cuco and Tunche were shocked! *Who did this child think she was?*

"We're going to need help from a friend!" they said.

So, the next night . . .

"Boooooo!"

Cuco hollered, and the bookcase rattled.

"Feeen feeen feeeeeennn!"

Tunche yowled, and the door shuddered.

"CAN'T YOU ALL BE QUIET?"

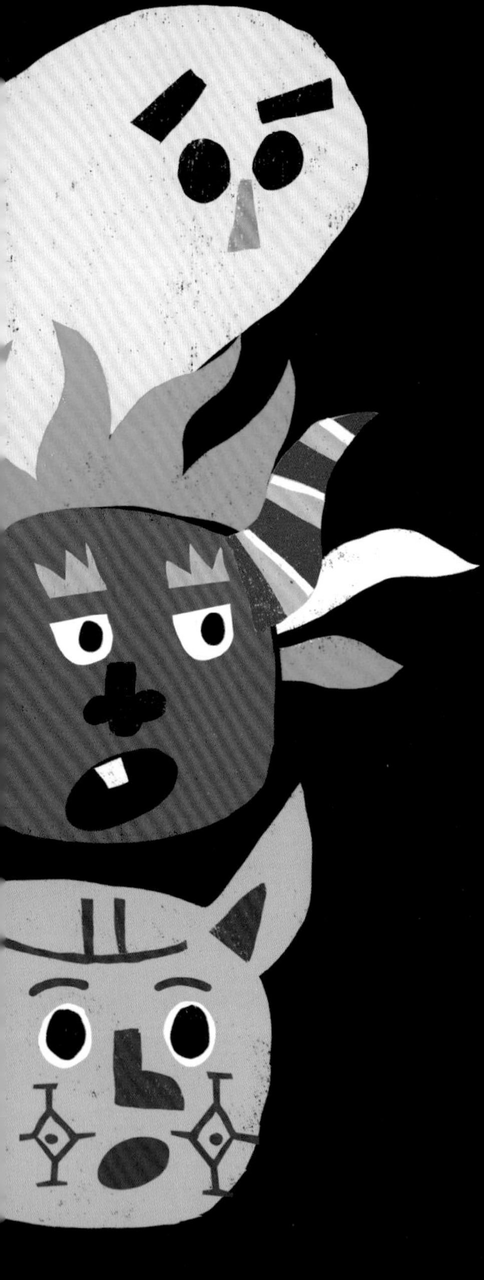

"DON'T YOU SEE I'M READING A BOOK?"

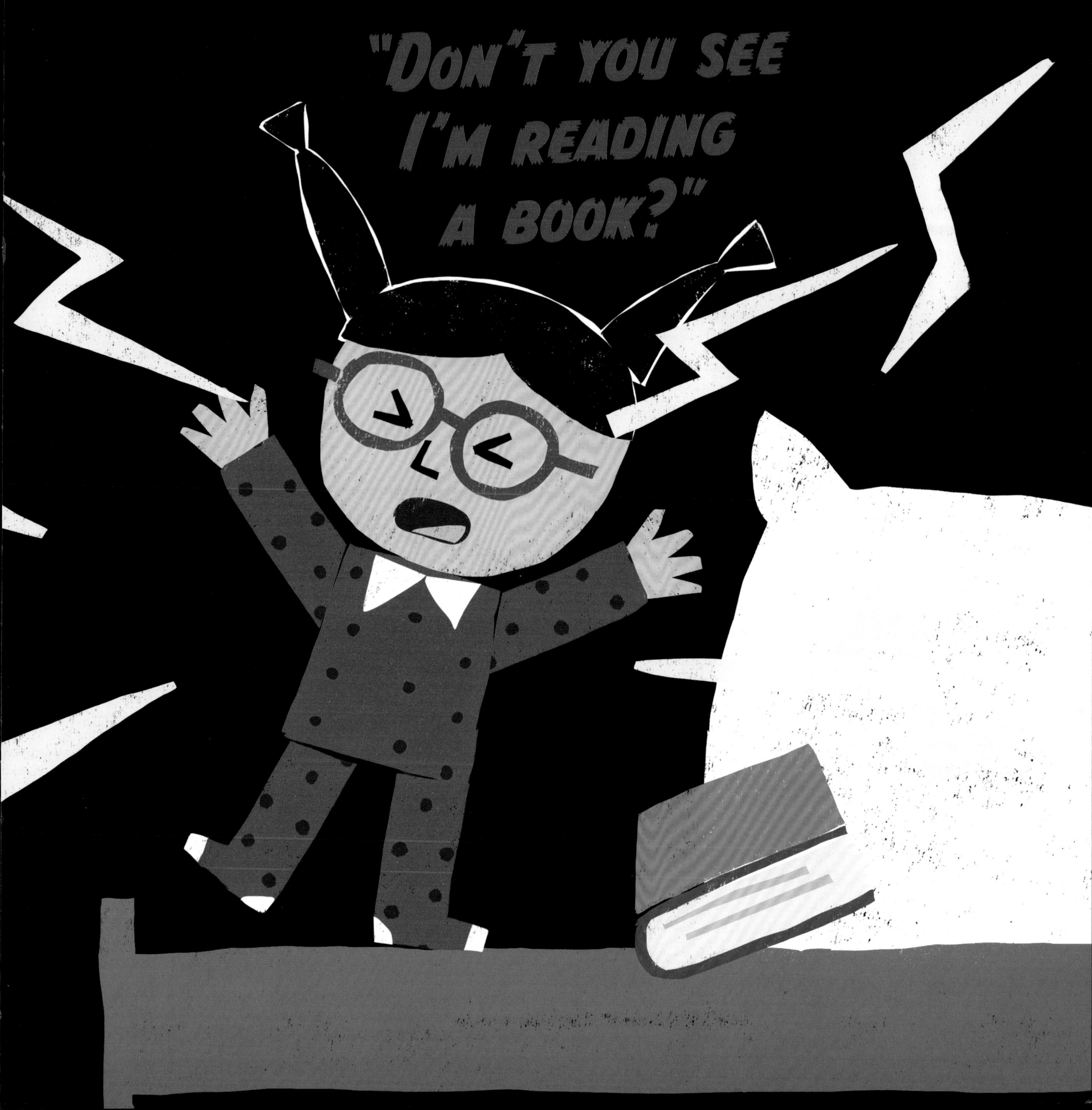

Cuco, Tunche and Supay poked
their noses up from behind Benita's bed.
And they saw...

Words floating on the page making sentences.

Sentences dancing on the page threading into stories.

Stories and pictures frolicking in front of their eyes, creating some sort of enchanting magic... Reading magic!

"But what does it say?" they begged to know.

Benita read them stories about faraway places,

brave monsters and humans...

... about rocket ships cruising in outer space and treasures in a secret chest...

and then...

bellowed Yanapuma, jumping
out from under the bed.

And Benita read on.

Meet Benita's Night Creatures

I'm a monster-like creature who likes to scare young kids. But don't be afraid if you ever see me. Just read me a silly story — not a scary one, please! — to tickle my funny bone.

Cuco
(KOO-koh)

I'm a ghost-like figure from the Peruvian Amazon. I enjoy whistling and blowing my freezing breath. But I'm not as scary as people think I am. If you whistle a catchy tune, I'll whistle along with you!

Tunche
(TOON-cheh)

I'm a spirit who lives on a tall, flat piece of land in Peru, Bolivia and Chile called the Altiplano (*al-tee-PLAH-noh*). I love wearing masks and costumes, but don't let my fancy looks fool you. I'm a big softie and I adore stories that make me cry. Can I borrow a tissue?

(Pssst, remember. Monsters aren't real! We are all just pretend.)

SUPAY
(soo-PAI)

I'm a huge cat-like creature from the Peruvian Amazon. My roar terrifies even the bravest people. But don't worry, I'm just like any other cat. I'll purr if you scratch behind my ears. Oh, and I love reading comfy mystery stories.

YANAPUMA
(yah-nah-POO-mah)

LEARN ABOUT PERU

Peru is a country in South America. Its capital is called Lima (*LEE-mah*) and is the largest city in the country.

Peru

Peru has three natural regions: the coast, the mountains and the rainforest.

Spanish is one of the official languages of Peru. Peruvians also speak over 40 different native languages, like Quechua (*KETCH-wah*) and Aimara (*ai-MAH-ruh*).

Easy Color-Coded Reference

Table of Contents

How to Use
This Handbook

A get-acquainted look at over 300 flowers and plants of interest to flower arrangers and indoor gardeners is provided in this handbook. Full-color photographs and step-by-step care and culture tips help make quick identification and give easy prescriptions for keeping flowers and plants looking their best longer.

Information is divided into quick-reference sections. These include cut flowers, flowering plants according to the seasons, green plants of all sizes, unusual plants, some popular favorites in the cactus and succulent groups and dried flowers, pods, grains and grasses for interesting and unusual arrangements. All sections are color coded with color-edged pages, matching an identical color coding in the table of contents. Green plants, for instance, are color coded green in the table of contents and all pages in the green plants section are edged with the same color to enable you to turn quickly to the section you want.

In addition, for the home gardener sections on bedding plants and bulb and root stock for all seasons are included.

Bachman's EUROPEAN FLOWER MARKETS® hope this handbook will help you get your indoor and outdoor flower and plant displays off to a beautiful start!

The Care of Cut Flowers

How to Make Them Last Longer

The beautiful flowers and plants you purchase from professional horticulturists are the product of careful harvesting and handling, so that they reach you in the best possible condition. A few suggestions for simple and effective care are offered in this handbook to help you keep them looking their best for the longest possible time.

When arranging flowers, follow these few simple care steps:

KEEPING FLOWERS HEALTHY

• The life of a cut flower depends on your keeping the water-conducting tubes (ducts) of the flower stem open. This is a simple procedure. First, be sure that the container is absolutely free of duct-clogging fungi by scrubbing it sterile clean.

• Secondly, cut off flower stem ends with a knife. Recent studies have shown that a slant or straight cut is equally satisfactory. Some woody stems will need to be split or mashed; others need to be dipped in boiling water or have their stem ends burned to seal in the milky substance. This will be noted under specific flower descriptions. Cutting of the stems will remove any clogging or drying that may have taken place during handling.

• Then remove any leaves that might be under water in the vase or container. Rotting leaves cause a build-up of fungi (bacteria) in the water.

WATER

• It is important that cut flowers always have sufficient water on their stems. The depth of water in the container should be a minimum of 3 to 4 inches. Warm water is preferred (about 100°F initially), because flower stems can absorb it more rapidly.

• Use a floral preservative in the water according to the manufacturer's directions. A good floral preservative is highly recommended for all cut flowers.

• If you do not use a preservative, it is difficult to eliminate the fungus problem, and it is best to recut the stems and change the water every day or two. When using a preservative, it is not necessary to change the water, but water should be added so there is always sufficient water on the stems.

HEAT AND LIGHT PRECAUTIONS

• Flowers should not be placed where they will be exposed to strong air currents. Hot sun and high temperatures (on top of TV, near radiators, etc.) also step up leaf and flower maturation and shorten useful flower life. You can slow down the process by keeping flowers in a cool place whenever they are not on display.

• Air conditioners remove moisture from the air which tends to dry out flowers. Misting the flowers and their foliage once or twice a day will replace some of the lost moisture. Always place flowers as far from air conditioner ducts as possible.

REVIVING WILTED FLOWERS

• If flowers should wilt, shorten the stems and place them in deep, warm water (about 100°F).

• If the stems tend to droop, lay the flowers flat on a piece of newspaper, stretching the stems so they are straight from stem end to flower head. The paper should be cut or folded so it is about 2 inches above the stem end and 1 inch above the flowers. Wrap tightly so stems stay erect and place in deep water. The newspaper will hold them firmly and also absorb water to keep leaves and flowers moist and prevent excessive evaporation of moisture. Usually 4 to 6 hours is required, but overnight is even better.

Cut Flowers... Year-Around Favorites

Flower favorites shown here are available year around thanks to modern growing techniques and production. Various sizes, shapes and colors make possible an infinite variety of imaginative arrangements with all of these popular flowers.

Carnations, Miniature Carnations, *Dianthus caryophyllus* — (Pictured below:) Clean flowers which never drop their petals, CARNATIONS are available in many natural colors, as well as several interesting tints. Both standard and miniature CARNATIONS have a spicy fragrance.

Chrysanthemums and Pompons, *Chrysanthemum morifolium* — All standard MUM (single large-flower) varieties must have their woody stems cut and then split to insure maximum uptake of water. A variety of forms, sizes and colors are on the market for your pleasure in flower arranging. Care should be used in handling many varieties of MUMS and POMPONS to prevent bruises to the flower, as they are subject to shattering when bruised.

(Shown from top to bottom at the left:)

a. Standard Chrysanthemums (Mums)
b. Disbud Chrysanthemums
c. Ball Pompons
d. Fuji Chrysanthemums
e. Solid Pompons
f. Daisy-type Pompons

(Pictured above:)

g. China Chrysanthemums
h. Button Pompons

(Pictured below:)

i. Daisy-type Chrysanthemums
j. Spider Chrysanthemums
k. Spoon Chrysanthemums

4

Cut Flowers...
Year-Around
Favorites

Daisies — Varieties of white and yellow DAISIES, commonly known as BOSTON DAISIES, are abundantly plentiful throughout the year, as well as several other brighter colors which are tinted. Bright colors are available naturally in GERBERA DAISIES and PAINTED DAISIES.

(Above:)

Yellow Daisies, *Anthemis tinctoria*

(Below, from top to bottom:)

Shasta Daisies,
Chrysanthemum maximum

Marguerite Daisies,
Chrysanthemum frutescens

Gladioli — Standard and miniature sizes are sold year around. A long-lasting flower, "GLADS" give a better appearance if the lower flowers on the stem are removed as they fade. The stems should be recut when this is done.

(Below:)

Gladiolus, *Gladiolus varieties*

Tea Roses and Sweetheart Roses—
TEA ROSE is a term commonly used to describe long-stemmed, large-flowering hybrid rose varieties. TEA ROSES are often very fragrant and are available in shades of white, pink, yellow, orange, red and occasionally, lavender. SWEETHEART ROSES are somewhat smaller than tea roses with an average stem length of 10 to 12 inches. They are available in the same range of colors as the hybrid tea roses.

(Below, from top to bottom:)

Tea Roses, *Rosa varieties*

Sweetheart Roses,
Rosa Cecile Brunner

Cut Flowers...
Spring Favorites

Anemone Poppies, *Anemone coronaria 'De Caen'* — (Below:) ANEMONES are happy flowers that brighten any arrangement; available in a great variety of colors with purple and blue shades the favorites.

Jonquils (Daffodils), *Narcissus species* — (Above:) This popular harbinger of spring is available in yellow, white, bicolors and even multiflowered types.

Freesias, *Freesia refracta* — (Above:) This dainty cut flower is grown from a corm. FREESIAS are very fragrant and have a light, airy appearance. As the flowering progresses, remove fading flowers as with gladioli.

Dutch Iris, *Iris hollandica* — Blue, purple, white and yellow are the principal colors available in IRISES.

Lilacs, *Syringa hybrida* — (Above:) Fragrant colorful LILACS have long been a popular vase flower. They will do best in arrangements if the stems are shortened and then split before being placed in warm water. Remove about three-fourths of all the foliage to keep the flowers from wilting.

Soleil d'Or Daffodils, *Narcissus tazetta* — (Below:) These popular spring flowers last longer if they are kept cool.

Peonies, *Paeonia* — (Below:) A choice cut flower, deliciously fragrant and a long-time favorite, PEONIES always look handsome in large vases. Varieties include singles, semi-doubles and anemone-flowered types.

Ranunculuses, *Ranunculus asiaticus* — (Above:) A double flower available in a rainbow of colors which resembles a rose. It is also known as PERSIAN BUTTERCUP.

Tulips, *Tulipa gesneriana* — Colorful and often fragrant, the TULIP is the most popular of all spring flowers. Horticulturists have developed varieties which are quite long lasting. They come in many colors, both solids and tricolors, as well as many shapes and sizes.

Cut Flowers...
Summer Favorites

China Asters, *Callistephus chinensis* — (Below:) CHINA ASTERS are large, long-lasting showy flowers, available in light and dark shades of pink, purple and white. Foliage decays rapidly and must be removed below the water line in the container at once.

Bachelor's-Buttons (Cornflowers), *Centaurea cyanus* — (Above, right:) Seen most often in blue, BACHELOR'S-BUTTONS add a cheerful note to any bouquet. They can usually be purchased in both single and double varieties.

Bells of Ireland, *Molucella laevis* — (Right:) A good unusual filler in many arrangements. Showy part is bell shaped calyx consisting of sepals which are part of the floral structure. Flowers are small, pinkish, fragrant. All foliage should be removed. The tall stalk with just the bell shaped blossoms looks gracefully elegant in arrangements.

Feather Cockscomb, *Celosia argentea cristata* — (Below:) Of the two types of CELOSIA, the cockscomb and the feather, the feather shown here is soft and graceful in a choice of muted shades in yellow, orange-scarlet and other bright colors.

Cosmos, *Cosmos bipinnatus* — (Below, left:) COSMOS is famous for its airy blossoms and feathery foliage, now available in many new colors.

Delphinium, *Delphinium cultorum* — (Above, right:) The stately spikes of the DELPHINIUM are a joy in a vase or large arrangement. They are most often available in blue or purple, but pure white, orchid and pink shades are available.

Forget-Me-Nots, *Myosotis sylvatica* — (Left:) FORGET-ME-NOTS are delicate little flowers, dainty and old-fashioned. Blue is the most popular, but they are also available in pink and white.

Gladiolus, *Gladiolus hybrida* — (Below, left:) "GLADS" are a summer-long favorite, available in many lovely colors in both standard and miniature sizes.

Marigolds, *Tagetes erecta* — (Above, right:) Some varieties are odorless, some have a pungent fragrance, all are long-lasting. Magnificent oranges and yellows in the color range; sizes from petites to stalks up to 24-30 inches.

Snapdragons, *Antirrhinum majus* — (Right:) These vertical flower spikes will open gradually from bottom to top. If florets are removed as they fade, the flower stems remain attractive.

Stock, *Mathiola incana* — (Below, left:) STOCK must have stem ends crushed, not cut for maximum intake of water. These are thirsty flowers, needing frequent addition of water to the container.

Strawflowers, *Helichrysum bracteatum* — (Above, right:) These flowers in their fresh state already look dried. They can be genuinely dried by hanging them upside down in a dry place.

Zinnias, *Zinnia hybrida* — (Below:) ZINNIAS range from little button varieties to huge cactus-flowered types in a range of exciting colors from pale pastels to riotous reds, oranges . . . even lavenders and greens!

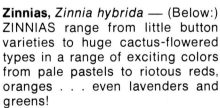

Cut Flowers...
Exotic and Tropical

Flowers to Wear

Anthurium, *Anthurium andraenum* — (Below, left:) This is the true tropical and must not be refrigerated. ANTHURIUM is very thirsty, and is considered one of the longest-lasting of all cut flowers.

Birds-of-Paradise, *Strelitzia reginae* — (Above, right:) As the blossom emerges from its sheath, it resembles a bird's crest, making the flower cluster even more large and colorful.

Cymbidium Orchids, *Cymbidium* — (Left:) Sprays of CYMBIDIUM ORCHIDS have a delicate fragrance and airy appearance. Single flowers can be floated in a bowl of water as individual place settings at a dinner table. An excellent long-lasting cut flower.

Gerbera Daisies, *Gerbera jamesoni* — (Below, left:) GERBERAS are also known as Transvaal Daisies. Native to South Africa, but are now grown mainly in California. They are available in a wide range of vivid colors.

Tritoma (Red Hot Poker), *Kniphofia uvaria* — (Above, right:) A most unusual flower, a source of exceptional color and a striking addition to any arrangement.

Corsages should be refrigerated in their closed box or plastic bag immediately and kept at this cool temperature until ready for wear. After wearing, corsage flowers should be re-refrigerated with moist cotton or paper toweling placed over them (except for orchids.) Misting of flowers and foliage (except orchids) is also helpful.

Orchids spot if touched with water, so they should be refrigerated but not moistened when not being worn. All corsages should be worn with the stems down, as flowers grow. Some of the most exciting flowers to wear include:

a. Lilies-of-the-Valley,
   Convallaria majalis
b. Marguerite Daisies,
   Chrysanthemum frutescens
c. Stephanotis,
   Stephanotis floribunda
d. Carnations,
   Dianthus caryophyllus
e. Cattleya Orchids, *Cattleya*
f. Camellias, *Camellia japonica*
g. Roses, *Rosa*
h. Violets, *Viola odorata*
i. Cymbidium Orchids, *Cymbidium*
j. Pompon Chrysanthemums,
   Chrysanthemum morifolium
k. Gardenias,
   Gardenia jasminoides

Cut Flowers...
Filler Flowers

The supplemental flowers and foliages needed to make flower arrangements professionally complete include these favorites.

Baby's Breath, *Gypsophilia paniculata* — (Left:) Light and dainty. Also popular in dried form.

German Statice, *Limonium sinuatum* — (Left:) STATICE can be used fresh or dried.

Heather, *Erica* — (Left:) Long-lasting, with dainty foliage.

Flowering Branches

Flowering branches open rapidly in a warm, humid room. When the blossoms fall, the dry, arching branch is also interesting and ornamental.

Acacia, *Acacia* — (Below, left:) Delicate, yellow-flowered.

Forsythia, *Forsythia* — (Above, right:) Bright, yellow-flowered background or frame for large arrangements.

Pussy Willows, *Salix caprea* — (Left:) PUSSY WILLOWS can be sprayed or dipped in color for interesting effects. For larger blooms ask for FRENCH PUSSY WILLOWS.

For the Christmas Season

Coniferous Evergreen Branches and Boughs. Evergreens at Christmas are prized for their long-lasting quality and for their delicious fragrance. DOUGLAS FIR is one of the longest lasting. (Above:)

a. White Pine, *Pinus strobus*
b. Balsam Fir, *Abies balsamea*
c. Red Cedar, *Juniperus virginiana*
d. Juniper, *Juniperus*

Not pictured:

Douglas Fir, *Pseudotsuga taxifolia*

English Holly, *Ilex aquifolium* — (Below:) Brightly-colored berries and glossy foliage for swatches, wreaths, table decorations and arrangements.

Mistletoe, *Phoradendron flavescens* — (Right:) Tie a sprig of MISTLETOE anywhere overhead, use it as a package trim, give it as a symbol of peace, as well as love.

Greens and Foliages

Green foliages in arrangements are an interesting contrast to bright flowers.

a. Scotch Broom, *Cytisus scoparius*

b. Huckleberry, *Vaccinium ovatum*
c. Salal (Lemon Foliage), *Gaultheria shallon*
d. Pittosporum, *Pittosporum tobira*

Foliages b, c and d give a massive appearance to arrangements.

e. Sprengeri Fern, *Asparagus sprengeri*

Use where a gracefully-drooping effect is desired.

f. Lycopodium (Hawaiian Staghorn Clubmoss), *Lycopodium cernuum*

A light, airy, upright green.

g. Boxwood, *Buxus sempervirens*
h. Eucalyptus, *Eucalyptus pulverulenta*

Foliages g and h are medium-textured.

i. Leatherleaf Fern (Baker's Fern), *Dryopteris erythrosora*

Bold, glossy, deep green foliage.

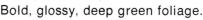

The Care of Flowering House Plants

How to keep them looking their beautiful best for the longest possible time.

Flowering house plants can be killed by too much attention! Tender loving care must be kept within bounds, so it is important to know something about the plants' individual needs for both day and night temperature, light, moisture and humidity. Most plants can manage to live in an unfavorable environment for a while. When they are given a special place in the home which is compatible to their needs, they will give more pleasure much longer.

LIGHT:
• Most flowering plants require some sunlight, preferably mid-day or afternoon sun. Diffused light or indirect light preferred by some varieties (as noted on succeeding pages) can be controlled with sheer draperies, or by changing the location.

TEMPERATURE:
• Most flowering plants need 10° F lower at night than during the day. When this is not provided, the food supplies in the plant will be used prematurely, shortening the useful life of the blossoms. The AFRICAN VIOLET is the principal exception.

WATER:
• Overwatering or letting a plant stand in water is to invite trouble. After the individual water requirements of a plant are met (these are noted in succeeding pages with individual species), the saucer in which the pot sets should be emptied of excess water. Saturated soil causes leaves to turn yellow and fall and more seriously, may cause roots to rot.
• Frequency of watering depends on the plant, room temperature, air circulation and type of pot. Clay pots lose moisture through the sides and need more frequent watering than plastic or glazed pots. Pots without drainage are hard to water, and must never be overwatered. Soil should always be dry to the touch in any container without drainage before applying additional water.

1. When watering, always apply enough water to wet all of the soil and have a little run out the drainage opening to avoid salt buildup in the soil. Roots will not grow in all of the soil if only a portion of the soil is wetted.
2. Pots should never stand in water when the soil is wet.
3. Watering when the "soil is still moist" means the soil is less moist than when first watered, but not yet dry on the surface.
4. Watering when the "soil surface is starting to dry" means the surface shows some dry particles but is still a bit moist to the touch.

In describing the best watering habits for each plant one of the four categories listed below will be used.

Water when:
  Soil is still moist
  Soil surface is starting to dry
  Soil is dry to the touch
  Soil has been dry a day or two (can be longer for many decorative green plants)

• Foliage, especially ORCHIDS, FERNS and GARDENIAS, can be moistened with a syringe or mister. Commercial misters, now available, or commonly-used sprinklers used for dampening clothes, do this job effectively. Hard (alkaline) water may leave a white residue on the foliage.

HUMIDITY:
• Moisture in the atmosphere (humidity) is needed by most plants and can be provided by:
a. Humidifiers in the home.
b. Placing plants on a gravel-filled tray where the water level is just below the bottom of the pot. Gravel in the tray makes it unnecessary to empty excess water, which then becomes a source of humidity.
c. Pans of water can be hung behind upright-type radiators.

FERTILIZER:
• Feeding flowering house plants should be done on a regular schedule, using a mixture prepared scientifically for house plants. Follow directions on the package to determine the concentration of the fertilizer solution to apply.
• Plants must not be fertilized when the soil is dry.
• Most plants have a semi-dormant period in the winter and should not be fertilized or watered as much as when in active growth. Overfeeding usually produces excessive leaf growth and fewer blossoms, or may eventually slow growth and injure roots.

The following plant descriptions include:
H. Height of plant
T. Temperatures preferred day and night
L. Light requirements
W. Water (moisture) requirements
F. Fertilizer schedule

Flowering Plants
Year-Around Favorites

African Violets, *Saintpaulia ionantha* — (Left:)

H. 4-8 inches
T. 65°-70° at night, 70°+ day
L. Bright, diffused, no direct sun except in the mornings
W. Water with tepid water when soil surface is starting to dry. Soil must always drain freely.
F. Monthly with good all-purpose house plant mixture.

ADDITIONAL HOME CARE TIPS:

When AFRICAN VIOLETS receive too much light, they will bloom freely, but will have pale, hardened foliage; with insufficient light, they will produce abundant foliage and few blossoms.

Pots should be turned frequently to maintain symmetrical growth.

Spraying with *tepid* water will wash dust from the foliage. Avoid getting water on the flowers, if possible. Cold water on the foliage or water on leaves in direct sun will cause yellow leaf spotting. The side shoots or little crowns should be removed so the plant remains with a single crown for maximum bloom.

Remove faded blossoms to keep the plant in bloom 12 months a year. It does not need a rest period. When the plant appears too large for the pot, it should be replanted in a larger container to encourage continued growth.

Rieger™ Begonias, *Begonia hybrid* — (Below:)

H. 10-15 inches
T. 60° at night, 70° day (normal household temperature)
L. Sun or light shade in the North; light to moderate shade in the South.
W. When soil is still moist.
F. Monthly

CHARACTERISTICS:

The Rieger BEGONIAS are a recent development with large flowers and the ability to flower over a considerable period. The variety pictured is Schwabenland Red.

Wax Begonias, *Begonia semperflorens* — (Above:)

H. 6-18 inches
T. 60° at night, 70° day
L. Sun or light shade
W. When soil surface is starting to dry.
F. Monthly, light feeding to help maintain a continuous display of blossoms.

CHARACTERISTICS:

WAX BEGONIAS are old-fashioned flowers, excellent for a window sill because they are not demanding in terms of care. WAX BEGONIAS are available in pink, white and red shades in several varieties. They all require pinching back (removal of growing tips) to keep the plants bushy.

Cattleya Orchids, *Cattleya varieties* — (Left:)

H. 12-15 inches
T. 60°-65° at night, 70°-80° day
L. Bright, diffused, with 4-5 hours sun per day. Some won't bloom if kept in continuous light for over 14 hours a day.
W. When growing medium is still moist. Mist foliage daily or place plants on a gravel-filled pan to increase much-needed humidity.
F. Apply a soluble fertilizer once a month at one-half the strength solution recommended for most house plants.

ADDITIONAL HOME CARE TIPS:

For the novice orchid grower CATTLEYAS are the best kind to buy, because with simple care they thrive in the average household climate. Good light is needed to insure good flowering. Adequate air circulation around the plant will improve its growth pattern. CYMBIDIUMS can successfully flower in the home but require slightly lower temperatures than the Cattleyas. PHALAENOPSIS, VANDAS and DENDROBIUMS are grown warmer.

Chrysanthemums, *Chrysanthemum morifolium* — (Below:)

H. 12-18 inches
T. 60° at night, 70° day. Place the plants in a cool place when not being used for decoration.
L. Bright light
W. May require water daily. Do not allow soil to get really dry or allow plant to wilt.
F. Seldom needed. Growers give CHRYSANTHEMUMS a rich soil in which to grow.

ADDITIONAL HOME CARE TIPS:

If mites or other pests should appear, the plants should be taken outside or to a well-ventilated area and sprayed with a recommended pesticide.

Flowering Plants... Spring and Summer Favorites

Chenille Plants, *Acalypha hispida* — (Above:)

H. 10-15 inches in potted form; 36-50 inches if used outdoors.
T. 70° at night, 75°+ day. CHENILLE PLANTS are tropicals, preferring the warm temperatures and diffused light of their native jungles.
L. Bright, diffused.
W. When soil surface is starting to dry.
F. Monthly.

CHARACTERISTICS:

CHENILLE PLANT is a real conversation piece. The long red catkins from which the name is derived are so unusual they hardly look real.

Fuchsias, *Fuchsia hybrids* — (Above:)

H. 15-30 inches.
T. 50° at night, 60° day. FUCHSIAS are cool weather plants and thrive best in these cool temperatures.
L. Moderate, diffused.
W. When soil surface is starting to dry.
F. Every three weeks.

CHARACTERISTICS:

FUCHSIAS are used both in hanging baskets and in pots. When filled with mature plants, the hanging basket of FUCHSIAS is spectacular.

Calceolarias, *Calceolaria crenatiflora* — (Above:)

H. 12-15 inches.
T. 50° at night, 60° day. CALCEOLARIA is a cool weather plant and does well, for example, on a glassed-in porch where it is cool, but protected from frost. Flower buds will not form and develop in temperatures above 60°.
L. Bright, but no sun. Bright sunlight might shorten the life of a CALCEOLARIA plant.
W. When soil is still moist.
F. Light, if needed.

CHARACTERISTICS:

CALCEOLARIA is a bushy plant with interesting little moccasin-type flowers. It is sometimes known as the POCKETBOOK FLOWER, a showy specimen that is used for indoor decoration in the early spring.

Cinerarias, *Senecio cruentus* — (Below, Left:)

H. 12-18 inches.
T. 50° at night, 60° day. If this preferred cool situation is provided, the flowering period of CINERARIAS will be prolonged for weeks.
L. Bright, diffused. Bright sun alone will shorten its flowering period, but strong diffused light (as through a sheer curtain) will open all the buds.
W. Requires considerable moisture every day. However, the pot must never stand in water.
F. Seldom needed.

CHARACTERISTICS:

CINERARIAS are brightly-colored bushy plants with broad-spreading daisy-type flower heads. The most commonly-seen colors are purple, maroon, blue, pink or a mixture of blue and white.

ADDITIONAL HOME CARE TIPS:

If the bushy foliage becomes too dense, some of the leaves should be removed . . . any that may have become discolored from overcrowding or some of the larger ones, starting at the bottom of the plant.

Geraniums, *Pelargonium hortorum* (Below:)

H. 12-24 inches.
T. 60° at night, 70°+ day. If room is hot and dry, however, leaf edges may turn brown.
L. Sun, as much as a sunny window can provide.
W. Moist, but dry between waterings. Lower leaves will turn yellow if it is overwatered.
F. Monthly during spring and summer.

CHARACTERISTICS:

GERANIUMS tolerate home conditions moderately well. They thrive on patios and porches. They flower best if root bound.

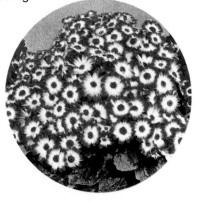

Gloxinias, *Sinningia hybrids* —
(Above:)
H. 10-12 inches.
T. 65° at night, 70-75° day. GLOX-
INIAS will not grow in a cool
situation.
L. Diffused light.
W. Use tepid water when soil sur-
face is starting to dry. Cold
water should never touch the
leaves.
F. Every 2 to 3 weeks with a good
liquid house plant fertilizer.

ADDITIONAL HOME CARE TIPS:

GLOXINIAS are a showy flowering
plant, related to AFRICAN VIOLETS.
They require a bit more light, however, and are not quite as sensitive
to overwatering.

Pots should be turned to keep
growth symmetrical.

Pacific Giants Primroses, *Primula
veris* — (Below:)
H. 10-12 inches.
T. 50° at night, 60° day.
L. Diffused light.
W. When soil is still moist.
F. Monthly, if needed.

CHARACTERISTICS:

This variety of PRIMROSE is not
irritating to sensitive persons.

Fruited Ornamentals...

Calamondin Oranges, *Citris mitis* —
(Above:)
H. 18-48 inches, taller where
native.
T. 50°+ at night, 70° day.
L. Bright to sunny.
W. When soil is dry to the touch.
F. Monthly with acid fertilizer ex-
cept when dormant.

CHARACTERISTICS:

CALAMONDIN ORANGES are very
pleasing both when in blossom (very
fragrant) and when covered with
tiny oranges. The fruit is tempting
but very acid-tasting.

ADDITIONAL HOME CARE TIPS:

The foliage should be syringed on
upper and lower leaf surfaces so
that the plant is protected from
spider mites.

Loss of flowers and fruit is often
caused by lack of light, too high
temperatures and incorrect
watering.

In the spring the plant can be pruned
to maintain its symmetry.

Ornamental Peppers, *Capsicum
frutescens* — (Right:)
H. 10-15 inches.
T. 65° at night, 75°+ day. Like outdoor PEPPERS, these thrive in
hot weather, but do not like a
humid atmosphere.
L. Sun or bright light.
W. When soil surface is starting to
dry. The soil must not be allowed
to dry out to the point that the
leaves wilt.
F. If needed, every 3 weeks.

CHARACTERISTICS:

Fruits of ORNAMENTAL PEPPERS
are hot, but edible.

Jerusalem Cherry, *Solanum pseu-
docapsicum* — (Above:)
H. 12-18 inches.
T. 55°-65° at night, 70°+ day.
L. Sunny or bright.
W. When soil surface is starting
to dry.
F. Every 3 weeks.

ADDITIONAL HOME CARE TIPS:

Leaf and fruit drop may be caused
by poor light, too much water, gas
leaks, or dry soil. With good care,
however, JERUSALEM CHERRIES
are long-lasting. The fruit is considered toxic. Plants should be kept
away from children.

Pineapple, *Ananas comosus* —
(Below, Right:)
H. 15-24 inches.
T. 60°+ at night, 70°+ day.
L. Sunny or bright.
W. When soil surface is starting to
dry. PINEAPPLE PLANTS can
be watered by trickling a stream
of water into the "cup" or top
of the plant. They like high
humidity.
F. If needed, very lightly.

Flowering Plants...
Seasonal and
Holiday Favorites

Potted bulbs that have been forced so that they will bloom early in the spring prefer coolness in order to keep their blossoms as long as possible. These colorful heralds of the spring season do not require fertilizer. The bulbs can be placed in the garden to grow again in their natural cycle, but considering the minimal cost of bulbs for fall planting outdoors, this is usually considered more effort than it is worth.

Crocus, *Crocus vernus* — (Above:)
H. 3-6 inches.
T. 50° at night, 60° day. Flowers will always last longer if the plants are kept cool.
L. Bright.
W. When soil is still moist.
F. Not necessary.

Daffodils, *Narcissus species* (Below, left:)
H. 10-15 inches.
T. 60° at night, 70° day. Blossoms will last longer if the plant is kept cool.
L. Bright light in northern climates, bright diffused light in southern zones.
W. When soil is still moist.
F. Not necessary.

Hyacinths, *Hyacinthus orientalis* — (Below, left:)
H. 10-14 inches.
T. 60° at night, 70° day. Blossoms will last longer if plant is kept cool.
L. Bright light in northern climates, bright diffused light in southern zones.
W. When soil is still moist.
F. Not necessary.

Tulips, *Tulipa gesneriana* — (Above, right:)
H. 8-14 inches.
T. 60° at night, 70° day. Blossoms will last longer if the plant is kept cool. When flowers are not needed for display, move the pot to a cool porch or basement.
L. Bright light in northern climates, bright diffused light in southern zones.
W. When soil is still moist.
F. Not necessary.

CHARACTERISTICS:

Tulips usually used for forcing are the early flowering singles and doubles, available in many colors and various heights. The shorter-stemmed varieties are especially suited for table centerpieces.

Easter Lilies, *Lilium longiflorum* — (Left:)
H. 24-30 inches.
T. 60° at night, 60°-70° day.
L. Bright light. Protect from strong air currents which shorten flower life.
W. When soil is still moist.
F. Not necessary.

ADDITIONAL HOME CARE TIPS:

After flowering is over, LILIES may be removed from the pot and set in a well-drained location in the garden when danger of frost is past. Planting depth should be about 6-10 inches. Under some conditions LILIES can bloom again in about 4 months.

Hydrangeas, *Hydrangea macrophylla* — (Above:)
H. 10-18 inches in pots, considerably taller outdoors.
T. 60° at night, 60°-70° day.
L. Diffused light.
W. When soil is still moist. During growing and flowering period HYDRANGEAS require frequent watering, often more than once a day. Do not allow wilting.
F. Not necessary in northern climates, monthly in southern zones where HYDRANGEAS can be planted in the shady garden.

Gardenia, *Gardenia jasminoides* — (Below, left:)
H. 24-60 inches.
T. 60° at night, 70° day.
L. Diffused light.
W. When soil is starting to dry. To receive needed humidity GARDENIAS must be syringed once or twice daily with room-temperature water when in bud and flower.
F. Monthly with acid-type fertilizer.

ADDITIONAL HOME CARE TIPS:

The fragrant flowering GARDENIA plant needs protection from spider mites or it will lose its leaves. Flower bud loss results from high temperature and low light intensity. GARDENIAS are usually long-lived, requiring a pruning in the spring to maintain their shape.

Miniature Roses, *Rosa hybrids* — (Below, right:)
H. 10-16 inches.
T. 60° at night, 70° day.
L. Sun or bright diffused light.
W. When soil is dry to the touch.
F. Monthly, except in winter.

CHARACTERISTICS:

Hardy MINIATURE ROSES are perfect for the sunny window. They must have a rest period in the garden during the winter. Wintering outdoors in the north is risky unless the plant is well protected by leaves or hay. When brought back indoors in the spring MINIATURE ROSES should be pruned to encourage new growth.

Azaleas, *Rhododendron cultivars* — (Above:)
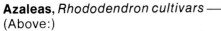

H. 15-24 inches in pots, considerably taller outdoors.
T. 50° at night, 60°-70° day. AZALEAS should be removed from the warm household and placed in a very cool place when not on display. When this is done, flowers may last for a month or more.
L. Bright, diffused light.
W. When soil is still moist. Do not let the pot stand in a water-filled saucer.
F. If needed, a light feeding at 3-week intervals with an acid-type fertilizer. Fertilizing is not necessary during flowering period.

Cyclamen, *Cyclamen persicum* — (Below:)
H. 8-12 inches.
T. 50°-60° at night, 60°-70° day. CYCLAMEN will not set buds at temperatures below 50°. If kept above 60° at night they have a shorter life span.
L. Good diffused light, bright sunshine in winter in the North.
W. When soil is still moist. Water from the side of the pot so water does not stand on the crown where leaves start. Never allow CYCLAMEN to wilt.
F. Every 3 to 4 weeks.

ADDITIONAL HOME CARE TIPS:
Blasting (drying or withering) of buds may be due to dry air, lack of soil moisture, insufficient light or cyclamen mites. Leaves may yellow quickly following severe wilting of plants.

Poinsettia, *Euphorbia pulcherrima* — (Above:)
H. 18-30 inches.
T. 65° at night, 70°+ day.
L. Bright, diffused light or sun.
W. When soil surface is starting to dry.
F. Usually not necessary.

CHARACTERISTICS:
The huge colored bracts of this showy Christmas flower look like leaves. The flowers are actually the tiny yellow centers nestled in the center of the brilliant color. Modern varieties in red, pink and white are hardier than those of past years; they do not lose foliage and bracts if exposed temporarily to drafts.

Christmas Cactus, *Schlumbergera bridgesii* — (Below:)
H. 6-15 inches.
T. 65° at night, 70°+ day.
L. Bright, diffused light, or place in an east window.
W. Evenly moist until the buds begin to form, then reduce until flowering is finished.
F. Light monthly.

ADDITIONAL HOME CARE TIPS:
CHRISTMAS CACTUS should be given short days, beginning the first of October, to bring them into flower for the holidays. Cover the plant so light does not reach it from 6 p.m. until 7 a.m. until buds form. Covering is no longer needed after this time. Short days are not necessary at 55° night temperature. No flower buds will form at night temperature of 70° and above.

Normal watering should be started as soon as new growth appears in the spring or after flowering is finished.

For an especially effective display CHRISTMAS CACTUS can be used as a hanging pot plant.

Kalanchoe, *Kalanchoe blossfeldiana* — (Above:)
H. 8-24 inches. The dwarf form of KALANCHOE is much more compact than the taller varieties.
T. 65° at night, 70° day.
L. Sun or bright diffused light.
W. When soil surface is starting to dry.
F. Lightly at monthly intervals, if needed.

Amaryllis, *Hippeastrum vittatum* — (Below:)
H. 18-30 inches.
T. 60° at night, 70° day. These are normal household temperatures. Plants will be stockier if the top temperature range is 65°.
L. Sun or bright light.
W. When soil is starting to dry.
F. Monthly.

ADDITIONAL HOME CARE TIPS:
AMARYLLIS has always been a conversation piece with its huge blooms topping 18 to 30-inch stalks with little or no foliage.

AMARYLLIS bulbs should be planted in a pot 2 inches larger in diameter than the bulb. The bulb should be at least a third above the soil level in the pot. Water should be given freely from initial growth to flowering.

At blooming time or shortly thereafter, foliage will appear. AMARYLLIS bulbs can also be grown in the garden for the summer and returned to the house for flowering in the winter.

No rest period is required. Plants grown continually will flower more frequently.

Foliage Plants
Identification and Care

LIGHT REQUIREMENTS

• Most foliage plants cannot tolerate direct sun, but thrive in indirect, diffused light in varying distances from the windows. This simulates the tropical or subtropical light under the tree cover in their native areas.

• It is possible to grow some house plants in dim light if they can be given periods of more light to recuperate.

WATER AND HUMIDITY

• Moisture requirements vary considerably and are noted under individual species. Generally, very few foliage plants will tolerate a soggy, wet soil. If a saucer is used under the pot, it should be drained within 2 hours after watering.

• Needed humidity can be obtained by frequent syringing or spraying of the foliage. Humidity can also be increased by placing pots of green plants in a pan of pebbles so that excess water which drains out can evaporate around the plants.

• Plants which are kept indoors from year to year should have foliage cleaned periodically by wiping it with a damp cloth. They may also be placed in the bathtub and given a hard shower with room temperature water. This will serve to remove, along with dust, most insects which might be present and any accumulation of salts left by evaporating water. An alkali residue may appear on the leaves after washing. A good leaf polish will improve plant appearance.

TEMPERATURE

• Home temperatures are generally satisfactory for foliage plants if they are maintained between 65° and 75°. Air conditioning can be tolerated if plants are not too close to the vents.

HEALTH CARE: PRUNING AND FERTILIZING

• Regular pruning is needed to keep many foliage plants within bounds and to encourage a bushy growth. Vines, especially, need this care to keep them in balance with their totem poles.

• Very light feeding with a soluble plant food labeled for house plants is best for foliage plants. The object is to keep plants in good condition, but to prevent excessive growth which frequent fertilization would encourage. Water ⅓ as often as you would if you desired maximum growth to encourage limited stocky growth.

The plant descriptions which follow include:

H. Height of plant
T. Temperatures preferred night and day
L. Light requirements
W. Water (moisture) requirements
F. Fertilizer schedule

Green Plants...
Large, Decorative
Plants

These large green plants are show-pieces, striking as an interior decor if they are given plenty of display space.

1. Neanthe Bella Palm,
Chamaedorea elegans bella

H. 2-4 feet.
T. 65° at night, 75° day.
L. Moderate diffused.
W. When soil surface is starting to dry.
F. Monthly.

2. Red-Margined Dracaena,
Dracaena marginata

H. 2-8 feet.
T. 65° at night, 75° day.
L. Moderate diffused.
W. When soil is dry to the touch.
F. Monthly.

3. Rubber Plant, Showy
Ficus elastica decora

H. 2-10 feet.
T. 60° at night, 75° day.
L. Bright diffused.
W. When soil is dry to the touch.
F. Monthly.

4. Bamboo Palm,
Chamaedorea erumpens

H. 4-8 feet.
T. 65° at night, 75° day.
L. Dimly lighted areas.
W. When soil surface is starting to dry.
F. Monthly.

5. Norfolk Island Pine,
Araucaria excelsa

H. 1-10 feet.
T. 60° at night, 70° day.
L. Bright diffused.
W. When soil surface is starting to dry.
F. Monthly.

6. Finger Aralia,
Dizygotheca elegantissima

H. 1-6 feet.
T. 60° at night, 75° day.
L. Bright diffused.
W. When soil surface is starting to dry.
F. Monthly.

7. Fiddleleaf Fig,
Ficus lyrata (pandurata)

H. Tree form.
T. 65° at night, 75° day.
L. Moderate diffused.
W. When soil surface is starting to dry.
F. Every two months.

8. Podocarpus, Southern Yew
Podocarpus macrophyllus maki

H. 2-10 feet.
T. 50° at night, 70° day.
L. Tolerant of dim sunlight.
W. When soil surface is starting to dry.
F. Monthly.

9. Dracaena,
Dracaena deremensis warnecki

H. 2-8 feet.
T. 65° at night, 75° day.
L. Moderate diffused.
W. When soil has been dry a day or two. Prefers dry side.
F. Monthly.

10. Australian Umbrella Tree,
Schefflera (Brassaia actino-phylla)

H. 2-10 feet.
T. 60° at night, 70° day.
L. Moderate diffused.
W. When soil has been dry a day or two.
F. Monthly.

11. Variegated Rubber Plant,
Ficus elastica doescheri

H. 2-8 feet.
T. 60° at night, 75° day.
L. Moderate diffused.
W. When soil is dry to the touch.
F. Monthly.

Green Plants... Medium-Sized and Colorful Foliage

This group of plants is a striking contrast to totally green foliages. Although tropical in origin, these plants do not require as much difference in nighttime and daytime temperatures as flowering plants do. The colorful leaves of this plant group require regular cleaning with a damp cloth. Less vigorous-growing forms are excellent for planters and dish gardens.

Dieffenbachias are especially tolerant of home environments, requiring less light and moisture than the others. Over-watering should be avoided!

1. Dumb Canes,
Dieffenbachia amoena

H. 2-5 feet.
T. 60° at night, 70° day.
L. Moderate diffused.
W. When soil has been dry for a day or two.
F. Monthly.

2. Dumb Cane Perfection,
Dieffenbachia picta var. 'Perfection'

H. 2-6 feet.
T. 65° at night, 75° day.
L. Moderate diffused.
W. When soil has been dry a day or two.
F. Monthly.

3. Dumb Cane Rudolph Roehrs,
Dieffenbachia picta var. 'Rudolph Roehrs'

H. 2-6 feet.
T. 65° at night, 75° day.
L. Moderate diffused.
W. When soil has been dry a day or two.
F. Monthly.

Crotons of all foliage plants will take full sun or bright diffused light. Leaves which develop in the sunlight are more highly-colored than those which are shaded. Many different patterns and colors of leaves often appear on one plant. CROTONS, however, cannot stand sharp changes in temperatures, which will cause them to lose their leaves very quickly.

4. Croton Bravo,
Codiaeum variegatum pictum

H. 3-10 feet.
T. 70° at night, 85° day.
L. Sun or bright diffused light.
W. When soil surface is starting to dry.
F. Sparingly every 3 months.

5. Variegated Crotons,
Codiaeum variegatum pictum

H. 2-5 feet.
T. 70° at night, 85° day.
L. Sun or bright diffused light.
W. When soil surface is starting to dry.
F. Sparingly every 3 months.

6. Variegated Aralia,
Polyscias balfouriana marginata or Aralia balfouriana

H. 2-4 feet.
T. 65° at night, 75° day.
L. Moderate diffused.
W. When soil surface is starting to dry.
F. Monthly.

7. Aphelandras,
Aphelandra squarrosa var. 'Dania'

H. 1-2 feet.
T. 65° at night, 75° day.
L. Bright diffused.
W. When soil is still moist.
F. Monthly.

8. Croton Elaine,
Codiaeum variegatum pictum

H. 3-10 feet.
T. 70° at night, 85° day.
L. Sun or bright diffused light.
W. When soil surface is starting to dry.
F. Sparingly every 3 months.

Philodendrons

This enormous family of plants is composed chiefly of climbers. A bark slab or pole is provided to simulate support originally offered by jungle trees. PHILODENDRONS should be pruned and kept on the dry side to control exuberant growth. In addition to watering as described below a humid atmosphere should also be provided. Foliage can be kept clean by wiping with skimmed milk.

H. Vines, except for SELLOUM which reaches a height of 3 feet.

T. 65° at night, 75° day.

L. Dim light, except for SPLIT-LEAF which must have more light or the leaves will not split.

W. Water when the top of the soil feels dry. Overwatering increases the rate of growth. Allow soil to remain dry for several days before watering to limit growth.

F. Monthly.

(Below, right:)

a. Philodendron,
Philodendron laciniatum

b. Emerald Queen,
Philodendron hybrid

c. Split-Leaf Philodendron,
Monstera deliciosa

d. Philodendron,
Philodendron selloum

e. Fiddleleaf Philodendron,
Philodendron panduraeforme

f. Heartleaf Philodendron,
Philodendron cordatum or *Philodendron oxycardium*

a. Rex Begonias,
Begonia rex cultorum
(Below, left:)

H. 6-10 inches.

T. 65° at night, 75° day.

L. Bright diffused.

W. When soil surface is starting to dry. Foliage should be kept dry.

F. Monthly.

CHARACTERISTICS:

The large, thick leaves of REX BEGONIAS are shaped and marked irregularly in fascinating patterns, each variety different.

b. Caladiums, *Caladium bicolor* —
(Below, right:)

H. 12-20 inches.

T. 65° at night, 75° day.

L. Moderate diffused.

W. When soil is still moist.

F. Monthly.

ADDITIONAL HOME CARE TIPS:

The showy foliage of fancy-leaved CALADIUMS may wilt if the pots in which they are planted have poor drainage.

Bromeliads, *Bromeliaciae* —
(Above:)

H. 12-24 inches.

T. 60° at night, 70° day.

L. Diffused light is best, although they will take full sun.

W. The "cup" or hollow in the leaf center should be kept filled with water. Soil should be kept moist but not wet as the root system is relatively small.

F. Seldom needed.

CHARACTERISTICS:

After the flowering season is past, the parent BROMELIAD plant will produce off-shoots and then die. These off-shoots may be potted in a light porous growth medium rich in humus.

Medium-Sized Green Plants...

Green Plants...
Ferns

In the 20's and 30's almost every home had a fernery in the parlor . . . a wicker basket filled with some form of Boston Fern. A revival of interest in these graceful foliage plants today makes them seem almost new and certainly interesting and exciting to grow. They are not difficult to grow if their requirements for humidity, tempered light and watering are observed.

Most ferns used in the home are tropical plants and grow best where humidity is high. If a heating system does not have a humidifier that maintains moisture level in the air at 40% to 50%, two things should be done for ferns: the foliage should be syringed daily and the potted plants placed on a frame over a gravel-filled pan. The fronds are delicate and will turn brown if brushed against. Repot infrequently because they are sensitive to root disturbance.

H. 8-36 inches.
T. 60° at night, 75° day.
L. Avoid direct sunlight except in the early morning. In southern climates this may be too much light. Diffused light is best, but even this will have to be watched, because foliage will turn yellow if exposed to too much light.
W. When soil is still moist. Avoid letting the soil dry out.
F. Monthly.

(Below:)
a. **Roosevelt Fern,**
   Nephrolepis exaltata roosevelti
b. **Boston Fern,**
   Nephrolepis exaltata bostoniensis
c. **Sprengeri Fern,**
   Asparagus sprengeri
d. **Leatherleaf Fern (Baker's Fern)**
   Dryopteris erythrosora
e. **Maidenhair Fern,**
   Adiantum pedatum
f. **Bird's Nest Fern,**
   Asplenium nidus
g. **Fluffy Ruffles Fern,**
   Nephrolepis exaltata
Not pictured:
Brake Fern, *Pteris cretica*
Holly Fern,
Crytomium Falcatum rochfordianum
Staghorn Fern (grows in sphagnum moss) *Platycerium bifurcatum*

Green Plants...
Vines and Ivies

The charm of vines and ivies is in their vigorous growth and petite size. Most of these plants are climbers by nature, but are equally at home drifting over the edge of hanging planters, mantels or ledge gardens or room dividers.
(Below:)

H. All are vining plants which can be pruned to control growth. POTHOS is an exception: see (g) below.

T. 60° at night, 70° day for IVIES; 60°-70° at night, 70°-75° day for the others.

L. Diffused light.

W. Dry between waterings for HOYAS, POTHOS, PEPEROMIA; when soil surface is starting to dry for the others.

F. Monthly.

a. **Grape Ivy,** *Cissus rhombifolia*
b. **Heart-leaf Philodendron,** *Philodendron cordatum* or *Philodendron oxycardium*
c. **Spider Plant,** *Chlorophytum commesum vittatum*
d. **Glacier Ivy,** *Hedera helix var. 'Glacier'*
e. **Hahn's Ivy,** *Hedera helix var. 'Hahn's'*
f. **Peperomia,** *Peperomia scandens*
g. **Gold Dust Pothos,** *Scindapsus aureus*

This vine is seldom pruned so the long tendrils can be trained to provide interesting foliage around a window or shelf.

h. **English Ivy,** *Hedera helix*
i. **Algerian Ivy,** *Hedera canariensis variegata*
j. **Gold Dust Ivy,** *Hedera helix var. 'Gold Dust'*
k. **Hoya,** *Hoya carnosa variegata*
l. **Hoya,** *Hoya carnosa*
m. **Wandering Jew,** *Zebrina pendula*

Not pictured:

Marble Queen Pothos, *Scindapsus aureus Marble Queen*

This vine with ivory colored, green steaked leaves should be grown at 70° minimum temperature with less water than the other Scindapsus.

Green Plants...
Plants for
Dish Gardens

Plants for dish gardens should be compatible in terms of requirements for light and moisture. Dish garden plants such as those listed below thrive in the normal home temperature range and with proper care will grow indefinitely in the dish in which they are planted.

a. Snake Plant,
Sansevieria zeylanica
- Moderate diffused light.
- Dry between waterings.

b. Nephythytis,
*Snygonium podophyllum
Tri-Leaf wonder*
- Moderate diffused light.
- Dry between waterings.

c. Chinese Evergreen,
Aglaonema var. 'Silver Queen'
- Moderate diffused light.
- Dry between waterings.

d. Neanthe Bella Palm,
Chamaedorea elegans 'Bella'
- Moderate diffused light.
- Dry between waterings.

e. Chinese Evergreen,
*Aglaonema (is usually
modestum*
- Moderate diffused light.
- Dry between waterings.

f. Prayer Plant,
*Maranta leuconeura
kerchoveana*
- Moderate diffused light.
- Water when soil is still moist.

g. Red-veined Prayer Plant,
*Maranta leuconeura
massangeana*
- Moderate diffused light.
- Water when soil is still moist.

h. Snake Plant,
Sansevieria trifasciata laurenti
- Moderate diffused light.
- Dry between waterings.

i. Variegated Chinese Evergreen,
Aglaonema commutatum
- Moderate diffused light.
- Dry between waterings.

j. Arrowhead Plant,
Syngonium podophyllum
- Moderate diffused light.
- Dry between waterings.

k. Variegated Peperomia,
*Peperomia obtusifolia
'variegata'*
- Moderate diffused light.
- Dry between waterings.

l. Watermelon Peperomia,
Peperomia sandersii
- Moderate diffused light.
- Dry between waterings.

m. Dwarf Snake Plant,
Sansevieria trifasciata 'Hahnii'
- Moderate diffused light.
- Dry between waterings.

n. Ivy-leaf Peperomia,
*Peperomia griseo-argentea
(hederaefolia)*
- Moderate diffused light.
- Dry between waterings.

o. Green Peperomia,
Peperomia magnoliaefolia
- Moderate diffused light.
- Dry between waterings.

p. Emerald Ripple Peperomia,
Peperomia caperata
- Moderate diffused light.
- Dry between waterings.

Dish garden plants are generally well-adapted to home temperatures. Individual cultural requirements are noted with individual varieties. All dish gardens have a primary need: good drainage. Pebbles, gravel or broken bits of clay pot with a small amount of charcoal placed in the bottom of the container before soil and plants are added will help establish the environment in which the plants will flourish. When plants show a lack of vigor, a light application of fertilizer may be given.

a. Sander's Dracaena,
   Dracaena sanderiana
- Bright diffused light.
- Water when soil surface is starting to dry.

b. Purple Passion,
   Gynura sarmentosa
- Colors develop best in bright light.
- Water when soil surface is starting to dry.
- Pinch to control growth unless used in a hanging basket.

c. Flame Violet, *Episcia cupreata*
- Bright diffused light.
- Water when soil surface is starting to dry.

d. Aluminum Plant, *Pilea cadierei*
- Bright diffused light.
- Water when soil surface is starting to dry.
- Pinch to control growth.

e. Australian Umbrella Plant,
   Brassaia actinophylla
   (schefflera)
- Bright diffused light.
- Water when soil has been dry a day or two.

f. Spotted Dracaena,
   Dracaena godseffiana
- Bright diffused light.
- Water when soil is starting to dry.

g. Coral-berry Ardisia,
   Ardisia crispa
- Bright diffused light.
- Water when soil is starting to dry.

h. Silver Euonymus,
   Euonymus japonicus argenteo variegatus 'Silver Queen'
- Bright diffused light.
- Water when soil is starting to dry.
- Pinch to control growth.

i. Golden Euonymus,
   Euonymus japonicus argenteo variegatus 'Yellow Queen'
- Bright diffused light.
- Water when soil is starting to dry.
- Pinch to control growth.

j. Boxwood, *Buxus sempervirens*
- Bright diffused light.
- Will tolerate cooler temperatures.
- Water when soil is starting to dry.

k. Podocarpus, Southern Yew,
   Podocarpus macrophyllus maki
- Very dim light.
- Will tolerate cooler temperatures.
- Water when soil is starting to dry.

l. Red Fittonia
   Fittonia verschaffelti
- Dim light.
- Water when soil is starting to dry, high humidity.
- Avoid chill drafts.

m. White Fittonia
   Fittonia verschaffelti argyroneura
- Dim light.
- Water when soil is starting to dry, high humidity.
- Avoid chill drafts.

n. Jade Plant, *Crassula argentea*
- Bright diffused light.
- Dry between waterings.

o. Moon Valley Plant,
   Pilea Dorothy Mulford
- Bright diffused light.
- Water when soil is starting to dry.

Green Plants...
Cacti and
Other Succulents
...Terrariums
...Bonsai

The green plant world is filled with hundreds of totally unexpected, exotic surprises, among them miniature desert scenes, tiny gardens enclosed in glass, plants that gobble up bugs or hamburger and dwarfed trees that may be six inches high and six decades old!

Cacti and Other Succulents — A hostile climate has forced these plants to find methods of conserving scanty rainfall. Stems do the work of leaves where a waxy layer, dense hairs, spines and scales lessen water evaporation through shading and reducing drying air movement near the stems.

Cacti need as much sunlight as possible and must have water withheld in order to survive. Moderate watering about once or twice a month is usually adequate to keep the root hairs from drying out too much. Cacti frequently will require repotting as they grow out of the tiny pots in which they are frequently purchased. When repotting, provide a sweet non-acid soil which contains ⅓ sand, ⅓ loam and ⅓ humus such as leafmold, compost or peat moss.

(Above, left:)

a. A Collection of ALOES and Other Succulents in a Small Dish Garden.

Plants which have similar requirements for sunlight and moisture can be grouped together as shown here. These particular plants need to be kept in soil which is on the dry side and in as much sunlight as possible.

b. Hen-and-Chickens *(Echeveria glauca)* in a Small Planter.

There are hundreds of forms and varieties of these interesting rosetted succulent plants. They spread by underground stolons or runners and soon outgrow their container. Blooms are produced from the larger plants which then die and the small plants (the chickens) grow up and replace them. HEN-AND-CHICKENS like sunlight and soil which is on the dry side.

Cactus Garden — (Below:)

A "sand box" cactus garden displays several specimens of these prickly little plants in the sandy environment resembling their native desert habitat.

English Holly, *Ilex aquifolium* — (Above, right:)

A small plant of ENGLISH HOLLY is an interesting innovation for the holiday season, and it will also grow as a house plant for most of the year. Berries usually are attached to specimen plants to make them pretty conversation pieces. HOLLY tends to dry out rapidly. Foliage should be misted and the soil kept moist, but not wet. Bright diffused light is preferred in a cool location.

a. Cushion Aloe, *Haworthia glauca*

b. Venus Fly Trap
Dionaea muscipula

A favorite of children, this bizarre little plant actually devours small insects, usually flies or spiders. If insects are not available, the plant can be fed tiny amounts of raw hamburger. The plant traps and digests its prey by the hinged leaves which operate like steel traps. Because of its need for high humidity, VENUS FLY TRAP is usually grown in a terrarium or in a pot equipped with a plastic cover. Bright diffused light is preferred.

c. Bonsai

Bonsai are examples of the oriental art of horticultural dwarfing. They are grown in shallow containers and despite their size may be several decades old. They require regular watering to keep the soil moist, but not wet. Root pruning, training and feeding are important. A good reference book, informative, well illustrated and inexpensive, which provides information about BONSAI culture is the *Brooklyn Botanic Garden Handbook,* Volume 9, No. 3, 1953 entitled "Dwarf Potted Plants As the Japanese Grow Them."

d. Assorted Cacti and Succulent Terrariums

This type of terrarium should never be covered, but left open to avoid accumulation of water. Cacti and succulents need a dry environment.

e. Assorted Green Plant Terrariums

A terrarium is a garden planted in glass which provides much of its own humidity and does not need the amount of water an open dish garden does. Light applications of water over the soil area weekly usually provide the needed additional moisture. Terrariums with tops, however, may require water only at intervals of several months, since the closed container makes its own "rain." Full sun should be avoided.

f. Variegated Jade Plant,
Crassula argentea variegata

g. Pinwheel, *Aeonium haworthi*

h. Red Velvet, *Echeveria harmsii*

i. Kalanchoe, *Kalanchoe millotii*

Kalanchoes are often grown only for their interesting foliage, but some of them are prized for their colorful flowers. They like bright light and are well adapted to home conditions. Periodic watering is essential because they are water-retentive. The soil should be allowed to dry out between waterings.

j. Gold Tooth, *Aloe nobilis*

k. Senecio, *Scaposus*

l. Crocodile Aloe,
Aloe brevifolia variegata

m. Felt Bush, *Kalanchoe beharensis*
See care instructions above.

n. Panda Plant,
Kalanchoe tomentosa

Dried Materials...

Dried grasses, leaves, flowers and grains provide the elements of "everlasting" bouquets. Most are available in muted earth tones, browns and bronze, although some varieties are dyed in brilliant colors.

After the drying process, these dried materials last indefinitely without ever requiring water. They tend, however, to be brittle and fragile and require cautious handling in arranging and in storing. A soft camel hair brush is a useful tool to clean leaves gently. Sturdier varieties of PODS, STRAWFLOWERS and SEA OATS can be carefully swished in suds, then gently rinsed to remove dust. Steam is good for air-dried materials such as CELOSIA and STATICE, because it removes dust at the same time that it softens stems and flowers so their natural shapes are restored.

Humidity is the worst enemy of dried material, causing it to disintegrate. To prevent humidity damage when materials are stored a small amount of silica gel added to the storage container will absorb moisture.

Shown above is a collection of popular dried materials classified as dried pods (P); dried leaves (L); flowers and berries (F); and grasses and grains (G).

Shown above also is an arrangement composed entirely of dried elements as an example of how these materials can be used. The numbers which follow identify the dried materials used in the arrangement and also those shown separately. Scientific names for the dried materials shown will be found in the index after the common name. See pages 32 and 33.

*Shown in the dried flower arrangement.
**Shown in the dried flower arrangement and also separately.
* 1. Sorghum (G)
* 2. Teasel (F)
* 3. Protea foliage (L)
* 4. Miniature Cattails (F)
* 5. Cardone Puffs (P)
* 6. Oak Leaves (L)
* 7. Wood Roses (F)
* 8. Lotus Pods (P)
* 9. Okra (P)
**10. Yarrow (F)
**11. Star Flowers (F)
*12. Sea Oats (G)
*13. Cecropia or Pond Leaves (L)
*14. Agave Cluster (P)
  15. Torch Ginger (F)
  16. Dock (G)
  17. Eucalyptus (L)
  18. Scrophularia or Figwort (G)
  19. Miniature Wood Roses (F)
  20. Lipstick Pods (P)
  21. German Statice (F)
  22. Buttons (F)
  23. Chinese Lanterns (F)
  24. Star Flowers (F)
  25. Happy Flowers (F)

Chives

Sage

Parsley

Rosemary

Thyme

Oregano

Sweet Marjoram

Pepper

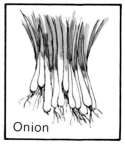
Onion

Tomato

Herbs and Vegetables...

Nothing equals the taste of fresh vegetables and herb seasonings grown in one's own back yard or in patio tubs. A few simple care considerations make possible a bountiful harvest. Instructions are given here for plot gardening. In smaller areas or in container gardening, the same rules apply, but on a reduced scale.

PLANTING TIPS:

LIGHT: Full sun except PARSLEY (see below).

SOIL CULTIVATION: Dig deeply and add humus (peat moss, leaf mold or compost) to hold moisture and encourage deep root growth. Add a phosphate fertilizer. When plants begin to grow, stop cultivating deeply in order not to harm feeder roots.

Most herbs and vegetables prefer a sweet (non-acid) soil, although TOMATOES will do well in either an acid or a neutral soil.

When to Plant: After the average date of the last killing frost for most herbs and vegetables.

Exceptions: ONIONS which are hardy and can be planted earlier.

PEPPERS, EGGPLANTS and TOMATOES must be held until the soil has warmed.

Set plants out in the evening if possible so they are not initially subjected to the heat of the sun. They can also be shaded with a piece of cardboard for a day or two until the roots are established.

WEED CONTROL: Mulch will help control weeds, or apply a pre-emergent weed control such as dacthal before planting. Covering the ground with black plastic and cutting holes in the plastic for plants prevents weed growth and also hastens warming of the soil in the spring. After plants start to grow, weeds can be removed by hand or with a trowel, hoe or small cultivators.

WATER: Water plants well before planting in the garden. For a week after planting keep the soil moist. Thorough watering of the garden may be necessary in periods when rainfall is not adequate.

Herbs and Vegetables

Kind	Height in Inches	Spacing in Inches
HERBS:		
Oregano, *Origanum*	30	24
Rosemary, *Rosmarinus officinalis*	72	18-24
Sage, *Salvia officinalis*	30	18-24
Sweet Marjoram, *Marjorana hortensis*	12	12
Thyme, *Thymus vulgaris*	3-8	6
VEGETABLES:		
Chives, *Allium schoenoprasum*	18	10
Onion, *Allium cepa*	18	2-4
Parsley, *Petroselinum crispa*	6-12	8
Pepper, *Capsicum grossum*	24-30	24
Tomato, *Lycopersicon esculentum*	48	26-50

BORDER AREAS

1. Ageratum,
Ageratum houstonianum

2. Alyssum Royal Carpet,
Lobularia maritima

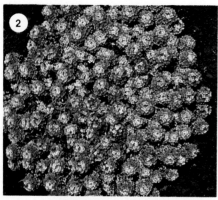

3. Portulaca (Moss Rose),
Portulaca grandiflora

COLORFUL PLANTS

4. Ivy Geranium,
Pelargonium peltatum
5. Pansy, *Viola tricolor*
6. Verbena, *Verbena hortensis*
7. Salvia (Scarlet Sage)
Salvia splendens
8. Viola, *Viola williamsii*

9. Petunia, *Petunia hybrida*

Bedding Plants

Bedding plants provide a season-long color display in the garden. Varieties are available from short and compact to tall and graceful for both sunny and shady locations.

Planting Tips:

Fertilizer: Enrich well-prepared flower beds with a complete fertilizer, or a phosphate fertilizer plus compost or dehydrated cow manure. A starter solution when transplanting will give plants an extra boost.

Weed Control: Mulch beds or hand cultivate with a trowel or small cultivator to control weeds and get the best show of blossoms.

Plant Care: Space adequately. Pinch the tops of those which become tall and straggly to stimulate bushy growth. Remove faded blossoms.

Water: Water each plant thoroughly when planting and keep soil moist thereafter. Do not rely on summer rain alone for adequate moisture.

INTERESTING FOLIAGE
10. Dusty Miller,
Senecio cineraria

CUTTING FLOWERS

4. **China Asters,**
   Callistephus chinensis
5. **Celosia,**
   Celosia argentea cristata
6. **Carnations,**
   Dianthus caryophyllus
7. **Marigolds,** *Tagetes erecta*
8. **Chrysanthemum,**
   Chrysanthemum morifolium
9. **Bachelor's-Buttons
   (Cornflowers),**
   Centaurea cyanus
10. **Calendulas,**
    Calendula officinalis
11. **Cosmos,** *Cosmos bipinnatus*
12. **Zinnias,** *Zinnia hybrid*
13. **Snapdragons,**
    Antirrhinum majus
14. **Gloriosa Daisies,**
    *Rudbeckia hybrid var.
    'Gloriosa'*

SHADY AREA PLANTS

1. **Wax Begonias,**
   Begonia semperflorens
2. **Coleus,** *Coleus blumei*
3. **Impatiens,** *Impatiens balsamina*

Tuberous Begonias (see page 30)
Begonia Tuber hybrida
Not pictured:
Browallia, *Browallia speciosa major*
Lobelia, *Lobelia erinus*

Bulbs and Roots

Planting Tips:

• In areas where the ground freezes, planted bulbs should have at least 4-6 inches of soil above them for protection. In very cold climates, a covering of hay will be needed. This should be removed in early spring.

• Bulbs planted in sandy soil should be planted deeper than those in heavier soil.

• A well drained location is essential.

• Generally, smaller bulbs are planted at shallower depths (4 inches) than larger bulbs (6 inches). A good rule to follow is to plant all bulbs three times the bulb height below the surface of the ground. DAHLIAS, 4-6 inches: GLADIOLI, 4 inches.

• Bulbs of tall plants which may topple in wind or rain should be planted deeper and in a protected area. Staking is also advisable.

• Tender bulbs should be dug after the foliage dries or is frosted, but before the ground freezes.

• Good soil preparation is important in a flower bed. Fertilize with humus (compost, leafmold, or peatmoss) or dehydrated cow manure. Bone meal or super phosphate mixed into soil before planting will usually produce larger flowers and better growth. Heavy clay soils should be treated with perlite or sand.

SPRING PLANTING

1. **Regal Lilies,** *Lilium regale hybrid*

2. **Rubrum Lilies,** *Lilium speciosum rubrum*

3. **Calla Lilies,** *Zantedeschia aethiopica*

4. **Yellow Cannas,** *Canna generalis*

5. **Daylilies,** *Hemerocallis*

6. **Gladiolus,** *Gladiolus hybrids*

7. **Anemone Poppies,** *Anemone coronaria var. 'St. Bridget'*

8. **Dahlias,** *Dahlia hybrida*

9. **Ranunculuses,** *Ranunculus asiaticus*

10. **Tuberous Begonias,** *Begonia tuberhybrida*

FALL PLANTING

1. **Allium,** *Allium giganteum*
2. **Tulips,** *Tulipa gesneriana*
3. **Daffodils,** *Narcissus*
4. **Madonna Lilies,** *Lilium candidum*
5. **Grape Hyacinths,**
   Muscari armeniacum
6. **Hyacinths,** *Hyacinthus orientalis*
7. **Paper White Narcissus,**
   Narcissus tazetta
8. **Crocus,** *Crocus vernus*

AUGUST PLANTING

9. **Bearded Iris,** *Iris germanica*

INDEX E
Common Names / Scientific Names